THE LEGEND OF
ESPERANZA BRIDGE
(THE TALE OF TWO CITIES)

ANDREA GUADALUPE GONZALES

Publishing Coordinator – Sharon Kizziah-Holmes
Cover Design – Jaycee DeLorenzo

Published by

Springfield, MO
Printed in the USA

ISBN -13: 979-8-9858089-0-2

DEDICATION

I dedicate this work to a very contemplative man and great writer, Ramon Miguel Cantu Ramírez Gonzales Mi Padre

And

Herlinda and Atanacio Ramirez, Mi Bisabuelos que me amaron tanto con su mirada

AUTHOR'S NOTE

My Dear Reader,

Esperanza Bridge (A Tale of Two Cities) is part of a trilogy. Writing this short story has proven to be a cognitive challenge. I found this short story completely necessary to lay the foundation of hope needed for this trilogy.

Life happens in layers. Since layers add to the depth and meaning of life, I feel like they can add to writing as well. *Esperanza Bridge* will be the backdrop for a love story titled *Las Palomas, Doves of Love and Peace.* This will be a love story. It will have characters that will be central to the third story. I hope to write each story in such a way that you could read each independently and feel the story is complete. You decide how many layers you wish to partake in. I am grateful for whatever number you choose.

All three stories have some true history in them. These history pieces just came into my awareness as I was formulating each story. It became evident to me to weave them into all three stories.

It is my sincere hope that each story will give you a unique way to experience yourself and know yourself better in some way. You are the best asset you will ever have. If I am able to help you deepen your relationship with yourself, then I am well pleased. You honor me with your eyes by reading my work.

I have taken certain liberties which I believe will enhance the reading experience such as italicizing certain words and capitalizing words that normally would not be capitalized. I believe we call it artistic license. Enjoy!

Thank you,

Andrea

ACKNOWLEDGMENTS

Julia, Jewlee, Amanda, Isaura, K. Appleton, Sue, Javier, Nina Maria, Sadie, Kristen, Brianna, Charlotte, Terri, Memo, Mrs. Hassell, Mrs. Hefner, Nancy Hope, Diana, Meridith, and K.E., all of you helped and supported me in ways you were aware of and in ways you didn't even realize. I thank you all!

An old, wide wooden rocking chair from the 1800's and a very colorfully woven blanket were roped off inside the *Esperanza Bridge Museum of History and Folklore*. Beside it was a plaque that read, "Whoever sits in this chair and wraps up in this blanket will be given a vision of *one* of the many legends of Esperanza Bridge."

Two teenage Latino lovers were walking past the rocking chair and blanket. They read the wooden plaque and they wondered if it could be true. They saw an old hickory bookshelf full of books next to the rocking chair with a sign that said, "These are the Legends of Esperanza Bridge." They picked up a book from the top shelf and walked over to the part of the reading area with an overstuffed couch. They began to read

THE LEGEND OF ESPERANZA BRIDGE (THE TALE OF TWO CITIES)

The Appalachian Mountains provide a pristine backdrop for stories and legends from long ago. Many generations of Appalachians have contributed to handing down a legend of adversity and peace between two villages. Both little villages were shrouded in illusion and saw themselves as "citics." This legend's birthplace begins in South America. It

is common among legends to blend the ordinary with the extraordinary, the usual with the unusual. This is such a legend.

In April of 1886, Herlinda and Atanacio Ramirez left the Andes mountains in Peru to follow the guidance from the Divine Spirit that they received from a series of mystical dreams. They were the kind of dreams that come from closing your eyes and making the distance between heaven and earth become smaller. In fact, it is said, the distance can become so small that the angels are said to deliver clues and revelations to those who believe that the Divine wishes to guide us all. The couple followed divine guidance in the way that one breathes air. North America's Appalachian Mountains were just the next steppingstone in their journey together.

Herlinda stood five feet tall and Atanacio called her his "plump little chili pepper." Atanacio stood 5'3" and she rarely said her pet name for him in public. Occasionally she would slip up and call him her "delightful tumbo," which is a sweet Peruvian passionfruit that has just a hint of sour.

Herlinda and Atanacio showed up in the Appalachians at the ripe ages of 67 and 64. Both were in perfect health at the time. They combed through the peaks and valleys of the Appalachians. They traveled for about a year before they found the area where they were guided by the Divine Spirit to make their new home. They both felt in their hearts that it was the right area they were searching for. Among all the u-shaped valleys, one stood out. It was the one situated between two villages. They decided to sleep down in the valley under the stars. As they snuggled together under a blanket, they prayed for confirmation.

The couple got confirmation in a peaceful dream. They saw tiny stones being tossed into a large pond, and the ripples kept going, becoming larger and larger. Herlinda and Atanacio knew it was their divine destiny to settle in this region. The first pebbles of the divine plan were being thrown into the water with faith. How large the ripples would become and how far-reaching was yet to be seen. Their faith and wisdom were the needed pebbles. While they slept, peace filled their spirits.

The next day they woke up to shouting in the middle of the valley. People were shaking their wooden rakes at each other, and pitchforks were being pointed at one another. The Ramirezes stared at each other in disbelief. They had never witnessed such rage and hatred by so many people. Herlinda and Atanacio did not realize just how deep the roots of bitterness really were until it spilt out onto the still meadow. Was this the valley that they were supposed to bring peace to? Helpless and shocked, they began to pray for help.

Suddenly, the northern wind began to make its way from over the mountain with great strength. Rain started falling so hard and fast that it hurt any exposed skin. The sun almost disappeared and so did the strife as everyone ran towards their village for cover. Their prayers were answered in the form of a thunderstorm. It poured for three days and nights. The Ramirezes gave thanks for the North wind and the rain as they fasted. They now knew that this was indeed where their new home should be. This was indeed a place in need of peace like Lamacia the Peruvian shaman had told them about. They began building their home in the valley in between the two feuding cities.

Even though they brought with them the wisdom of their people, it was balked at by others at first. As time grew, suspiciousness subsided. Trust began to form between the towns people as both little villages witnessed the couple's helping nature.

One little "city," *Esperanza,* which means "hope" in Spanish, was known for its finely, intricately woven blankets. The other little "city" was named *Puente,* which means "bridge" in Spanish. It had a reputation for very strong men who were masters at cutting wood at the exact perfect lengths for winter fires for cooking. Legend says there was something secret about the wood they cut because it would burn longer as if by magic. People from far away would come to the two little "cities" because of their talents.

Both little villages spoke English and Spanish in daily life. Yet, they were as far apart as the letter A is to the letter Z. The two shared languages, alone, were not strong enough to unite the two villages. The Ramirezes did not know why the two little villages had so much dislike for each other. There are many legends as to why there was so much disdain between the two. Regardless, it is safe to say a root of unforgiveness and misunderstanding could probably be found on both sides by the adults of each little village.

To the east of the couple's home was the little village of *Esperanza*, and to the west was the little village of *Puente*, both within walking distance. Children from *Esperanza* and *Puente* would often find themselves playing together in the vast forest that surrounded their village. In the forest, there was no division. *In the forest, they were all one*. It did not matter if you spoke English or Spanish. There was no brown or white. There was only green; the green of the lush forest floor that united their magical playground. They were one with the trees and all of nature.

They were playing in complete harmony. They saw their world through innocent

children's eyes. It did not matter if you were from *Esperanza* or *Puente.*

It was a custom that by the age of ten, few of these children played in the forest anymore.

Play gave way to work, as was common at that time. Sometimes while working, they reminisced of earlier times. Ultimately, however, the memories of childhood in the forest had only two destinations. Some of these memories became like seeds of dandelions blown into the mighty wind. The wind would carry the memories away, never to be remembered again.

The other children would take these memories and plant them deep into their hearts, where they would remain until they were old enough to become friends, lovers, or both.

Lovers who found each other in the woods playing as children would often move away from both villages as adults so their love could flourish. The lovers who did choose to stay because of the area's beauty would be forced to pick one village over the other to live in and would consequently leave the only hometown they had ever known. Their allegiance to the town of their birth was now called into question. They endured many unkindnesses and were considered traitors. Both little "cities" were unwilling to bend. There seemed to be little hope for the two villages being able to bridge their differences. Both little "cities" were blind to the irony of the meanings of their own village names; *Esperanza* being "hope" and *Puente* being "bridge."

Little did anyone know the disharmony was what the Ramirez couple came to mend. It was a believable destiny when you remember their last name is noted to have the meaning of counselor.

~ ~ ~ ~

One evening the Peruvian couple were sitting before a small dying fire made with the logs from *Puente*. They were wrapped up together in a blanket made by the people of *Esperanza*. The wind picked up from the south and a particularly woodsy smell wafted before their noses. It faintly reminded Herlinda of the time right before they left Peru. Herlinda and Atanacio began reminiscing about home and their identical dreams. They squeezed each other's hand as they remembered their dream.

Identical dreams are not uncommon among some lovers. Herlinda and Atanacio's dream had shown a sunny region they had never seen before with two villages. It was a breathtaking mountainous region painted with abundant trees and sparkling waterfalls.

The green tranquility would then be shattered by tiny crimson drops falling down onto the forest floor. Startled, they would look above

and see two doves colliding into each other again and again. The doves would violently peck at each other to the point of drawing blood. This would cause tiny drops of blood to fall. In the bright sun, they could see the doves were bleeding.

Then, as night would fall, the collisions between the two doves continued, this time bringing about teardrops. The discord between the two villages during the daytime had caused great sorrow to build up. Now the doves were crying. The moonlight would quietly catch this sorrow that was hidden in the darkness. Herlinda and Atanacio kept having this dream over and over.

They remembered being so troubled by the dream they went to see a shaman in Cuncani, Peru. The villagers of Cuncani were a remnant of the ancient Inca civilization. They had a reputation of being kind, helpful, and mysterious.

Herlinda and Atanacio had walked for two days and nights to reach Cuncani. As they approached the tiny village, the vibration of drums and flutes could be felt beneath their feet. The whole village was gathered outside of the shaman's house. The elderly female shaman, Lamacia, stood 4'9" tall and her hair fell down to her feet and dragged on the ground. She had been expecting them.

As Herlinda and Atanacio sat down in front

of the crackling fire, they were handed plates of food. They were also given cimarrón, the traditional Peruvian drink. The cimarrón was still hot and tiny little clouds of steam slowly rose up into the night air. These little clouds mysteriously parted as the neared the shaman, Lamacia. It was if the clouds were honoring her connection with the Divine Spirit. She gently smiled and did not speak. She nodded for them to get closer when they finished eating.

Herlinda spoke first and told of the doves violently colliding into each other and drops of blood falling onto the forest floor. After hearing this, Lamacia rose up from where she was sitting and gently took off one of the 13 beaded necklaces she was wearing. She threw the all white beads into the fire and the fire became small and calm. All of the crackling from the fire stopped as if by command. The drums and flutes were so faint; they were barely audible.

Then she unfolded a blanket containing herbs and other plants. She picked up specific items from the blanket and put them into a tiny sack. She then chanted three words in Spanish and threw the sack into the fire. The flames were now as tall as trees reaching into the night sky.

She then nodded for Atanacio to speak. He told her about the teardrops of the doves being visible by moonbeams. After hearing this, Lamacia seemed almost stumped. She closed her eyes and put her hand on her heart. Then she lifted her arms up towards the heavens and chanted in Quechua, an ancient language from the Incas. Atanacio thought he understood the words Peace, Strength, and Love, but he wasn't sure.

Then Lamacia took all of the black beads that were around her neck and flung them into the fire. The heat of the fire greatly intensified. Herlinda and Atanacio stepped way back from the fire as sweat poured down their faces. She then nodded at the drummers and brought her hand up to her waist. They began to beat their drums louder and the flutes quietly continued in the background. Then she lowered her hand and the drums ceased. Lamacia opened her eyes and grabbed three items from her blanket. In complete silence, one by one, she threw them into the fire. Each item elicited a different response from the flames. It was as if the flames were dancing, each with their own unique dance to the gentle music of the wooden flutes.

Lamacia spoke. Since she rarely spoke, the quiet music of the flutes ceased. She said, "The tears and the blood are both telling a story. The drops of blood illuminate the depth of pain and loss of vitality. The tears are tears of sadness felt by the Divine Spirit because of the belief in the illusion of separateness."

Lamacia confirmed that they were to leave Peru and go to a land they did not know because the doves were calling them to bring an end to the illusion of separateness. They were to bring peace to an unknown region riddled in conflict. Herlinda and Atanacio wanted to know how they were to bring peace. The shaman told them that it would organically unfold and to stay alert and look for a u-shaped valley.

That night they remembered deciding to leave the only homeland they had ever known to embark on an adventure that they were unsure of. As they slept under the stars they had always known, their dream changed. They both once again had an identical dream. This dream was new, and it was good. It was full of harmony. In their dreams they saw the two doves again, but that was the *only* thing that was the same.

Atanacio and Herlinda saw the two birds were again flying high above the trees with no blood or tears. The birds flew next to each other with grace. The moonbeams shone down and illuminated their perfect alignment. It was as though they were one bird, yet they were two. They were in perfect sync with each other. It was beautiful. It was peace. The two doves exemplified the two villages living in harmony and unity. What had once been an interaction of violent pecking, now had turned into an elegant ariel waltz.

As they fondly finished reminiscing about their journey, the fire burned itself out in *perfect timing*. Then another gust of wind from the south blew quietly carrying the whispers of their ancestors. Herlinda smiled at Atanacio and said, "My delightful tumbo, it is our ancestors reminding us of home."

Atanacio nodded and said, "Sí my plump little chili pepper, and they are reminding us they are always with us." Atanacio gently kissed Herlinda on the forehead as they went to sleep.

~ ~ ~ ~

As time passed, the people from both villages began to uncover the gifts of the two from Peru. In their dreams, the couple would see when the best time was to plant seeds. They were called upon for their Peruvian medicine of herbs and prayers. Sometimes, Herlinda could pierce the most hardened of hearts with her eyes of love. It usually only lasted, though, while in her presence. Atanacio could also pierce hearts of stone with his most loving, gentle gaze, and it, too, usually only lasted while in his presence.

As the people of both little villages became more open to what this couple had to give, it spurred another competition to begin. Each little village wanted them to move from their neutral home and claim their little village as their new home. Gifts started showing up at the door with no person in sight. Two gifts appeared the most, the beautifully handmade blankets that were warmer than the ones they had in Peru and the freshly chopped hardwood logs ready to be put on the fire for winter.

It was the people of *Esperanza* that brought the blankets. They also brought a secret elixir of all undisclosed ingredients to help the Peruvian couple acclimate to their foreign surroundings. The people of *Esperanza* refused to reveal the recipe. Herlinda and Atanacio tasted one familiar ingredient, honey.

Upon hearing about this, the people of *Puente* would not be outdone, so they too had a magical elixir with unknown ingredients. Again, the couple tasted one familiar ingredient, basil.

Little did any of the adults know their elixir was combined with the other. In their dreams, Herlinda and Atanacio were shown it would be safer if only the children knew this. Apparently, it took the blending of both elixirs for them to have optimal health. Their bodies were trying to adapt to not being in Peru. Mixing the two elixirs was a secret that they were told to keep from the adults by the Divine Spirit. At the right time, they would be guided to reveal the blending of the elixirs, and they were warned this would change everything.

Change was in the air, and it was about to befall the couple and the two little villages. The autumn leaves had not yet started to turn, but the air was crisp. This time of year was a very busy time for both little "cities" as they prepared to sell their blankets and chopped wood. There was not much time to spare within a day for anything else but weaving blankets and chopping wood.

The Ramirezes were befriending people from *Esperanza* and *Puente*. They asked both villages to assemble on a Sunday in front of their house. There was great speculation about this meeting. Like in most small "cities," people were very nosey. Rumors began to develop in the five days before the gathering. The Ramirezes had heard 36 rumors before that Sunday. None of them accurate.

The Ramirezes put out blankets for people to sit on and had made small fires with the wood. The people of *Esperanza* sat on the blankets and would not go near any of the tiny fires. The people of *Puente* refused to sit on blankets made by the people of *Esperanza*. Amongst such beauty of the Appalachian forests and meadows, the division was clear. It was very foreign to the couple. In the Andes, community flourished. It was a way of life.

Atanacio had made a small stage to stand on. It was made from the wood from *Puente*. He wrapped a blanket from *Esperanza* around him as he began to talk. He spoke *first* in Spanish and then repeated it in English.

Atanacio told the people that they were going to need each other in unexpected ways. He told them that *Puente* should give lots of wood to *Esperanza*. He instructed *Esperanza* to give many blankets to *Puente*. These instructions caused great grumbling from both sides. He then revealed that he and Herlinda's bodies needed the elixir from both villages to remain well. Most people were appalled that the elixirs were mixed.

Herlinda then spoke. She spoke in English *first* and then Spanish. Someone complained from the crowd. She gently said, "Mutual respect inspires great harmony." The people who spoke better English from *Puente* were grateful. The people who spoke better English from *Esperanza* were grateful. Then Herlinda revealed that they had once again had a dream. She informed the crowd that in March of 1888, there was going to be lots of snow. Both villages needed to work together to help build a bridge across the u-shaped valley. Atanacio told them it would be necessary to shuffle supplies back and forth more quickly instead of having to walk down into the u-shaped valley.

Most of the adults were angry and did not believe the Ramirezes' prediction. Work together? Snowstorm in March? The children, however, listened and believed. The people disbursed, shaking their heads. Most were refusing to build a bridge. The words "NEVER" and *"NUNCA"* could be heard from far and wide as it echoed throughout the valley.

The next day, the children began stockpiling blankets and cut wood in the forest. They built a shelter out of brush to help keep these things dry. The adults were still walking in outrage. They were secretly delighted to have something else to flaunt their dislike for one another. Both villages grew in resentment and outrage because each village thought their village was better than the other. Each village believed it would never need *anything* that the other village had to offer.

Their pride was so great that both sides refused to bring the couple their healing elixir. The children from *Esperanza* and *Puente* secretly brought their village's elixir into the woods. Herlinda and Atanacio would take turns retrieving it. These elixirs were not as effective as when the adults made it. There was also a marked difference in the taste and smell. Herlinda and Atanacio could feel the difference in their bodies. This made sleeping more difficult. Yet, they never spoke a word of this to the children because love often tries to protect.

For one week, the Ramirezes were ignored. No one from either village visited the Ramirez home until *someone* needed some type of help. People once again were open to receiving the gifts the couple had. As time passed, the two little villages witnessed many miracles being funneled down from the Great Spirit through the couple. Miracles come in many sizes.

Scorn for the couple began to fade and both little villages began giving their unique gifts to the couple again. The scorn each village had for the other seemed too deeply rooted to be pulled up. The Ramirezes would try to use their "soft power" to pull up these deep roots. Herlinda would say divinely guided things about *Puente* when talking to women from *Esperanza*. When talking to women of *Esperanza*, she would carefully weigh each word about the women of *Puente*. Herlinda was so gentle in her approach. It was as gentle as a feather and most people did not even realize the internal changes that occurred. Her soft power was so eloquent to behold.

Atanacio would use his eyes of kindness and the hidden qualities his eyes possessed when he was among the men from both villages. He meticulously would make mental note of men who needed more exposure to kindness and prayer.

It was mid-fall, and a few people from *Esperanza* and *Puente* imagined starting the bridge, but fear kept them immobile. One brave young man from *Puente* began with one piece of wood to build the bridge. This encouraged others from *Puente* to help. They would put in the extra work in the evening until it was too dark. Upon seeing this, it sparked the people of *Esperanza* to work on the bridge. The people of *Esperanza* refused to be at the building site at the same time. They got up earlier in the morning and would work on the bridge for a few hours in the morning. It was early winter when the bridge was done.

The bridge was a masterpiece of workmanship. The children and the Ramirezes could see its' beauty because they had the capability to see it. Legend says a few adults from each city could see the beauty too but kept silent. Fear can often cripple the tongue.

The Ramirezes called a gathering again. Once again, they laid the beautiful blankets from *Esperanza* on the ground, and they made small fires from the wood of *Puente* to keep the people warm. As before, both villages showcased their disdain for one another by refusing the gifts of the other "city." The people of *Esperanza* sat on *their* blankets as the people of *Puente* gathered around the little fires made from *their* logs.

The Ramirezes told the people that they saw in a more recent dream that the situation had become more dire. Atanacio spoke firmly and warned them that a "White Hurricane" was going to befall them all. The couple told everyone that they needed to store wood in their homes and as many blankets as possible. They recommended that the children handle the mediation of the blankets and wood. Legend says the Ramirezes encouraged each village to pray for the safety of all. They also encouraged each village to exchange other things as well. The Ramirezes had hoped to spark collaboration. There are conflicting stories about the amount of collaboration that actually occurred. The children handled the exchange of blankets and wood with ease and grace.

December of 1887 came, and the bridge was only used by the Ramirezes. January and February of 1888 came, and the children began using the bridge. Finally, March of 1888 came. Most people, with the exception of the children, believed it was all a ruse because signs of spring were abound. Mother nature was putting on her spring dress earlier than usual. Trees were starting to bud, and the temperatures were unseasonably mild. Both towns began to smell the beginnings of early spring.

This created a sense of even greater disbelief that severe weather was around the corner.

March 1st came, and *Esperanza* people grumbled about the whole idea of having to work together for nothing.

March 2nd came, and *Puente* people complained about how much work they had contributed to complete such a task.

March 3rd came, and they both griped about how they had shared wood and blankets.

March 4th came, and *Esperanza* and *Puente's* people began to jeer at the Ramirezes.

March 5th came, and *Esperanza* people were annoyed the Ramirezes could be so presumptuous to suggest that they had that such a gift to see that far into the future.

March 6th came, and *Puente* people were bored with the whole idea.

March 7th came, and *Esperanza* people were feeling an internal curiosity about the weather. Perhaps it wasn't so outlandish after all. The weather was unusually mild according to the old timers for this time of year. This seemed very odd to the weather watchers.

March 8th came, and *Puente* people could not fathom a white hurricane of snow.

March 9th came, and *Esperanza* people felt foolish for even thinking perhaps it was possible.

On March 10th, *Esperanza* and *Puente's* people were plotting how to burn down the bridge and make it look like the other side did it.

March 11th, both sides were going to burn down the bridge at dusk.

Both little villages were on *their* side of the bridge with torches. Disbelief in the prediction grew as the wind picked up and made the flames from the torches climb even higher into the evening sky. It was if the torches were giving a picture of the fermenting anger inside the people. Grumblings of anger could be heard in the cold air.

Suddenly, tiny little snowflakes began to fall.

The little embers of fire from the torches were dancing among the snowflakes. The tiny flakes were gently working together to begin to knit a beautiful blanket, a blanket of unity. Soon it was like a thin blanket covering the earth. The thin blanket became a medium blanket. The medium blanket became a thick blanket. The snowflakes were busy falling gently to create this new blanket.

Shocked and dismayed, there was dead silence in the air as the people realized it could be true. They began to scurry back and forth between the two villages to trade things before it got worse. They were in shock and awe. Many were still trying to convince themselves that the snowfall would not get past 7 or 8 inches. Yet, for some, their hearts now knew the prediction was true.

The Ramirezes knew it would be in the 11th hour before they would believe. It was late, but not too late. The snow began to slowly start pounding down onto the earth as if it were trying to convince everyone how harsh things would become. Many could now see why the Ramirezes had wanted there to be great generosity.

The people of *Esperanza* decided to give even more blankets than before but now they started tenderly wrapping eggs into the blankets. The people of *Puente* began gifting more wood with pieces of meat alongside the wood. This created a big shift in both little villages. Now the competition became which village could be more generous. Butter, milk, honey, and dried herbs were brought across the bridge. *Esperanza* and *Puente* gave the Ramirezes huge quantities of the healing elixirs. Legend says there were magical things exchanged too, but that's another story.

Daylight hours were consumed with both villages exchanging important supplies, and talk began about celebrating each other's strengths. Legend says that there were even occasional smiles exchanged at each other while crossing the bridge. The bridge that was going to be burnt down was now helping each village survive. The villagers from *Esperanza* and *Puente* decided to hold a big picnic in the field when the weather was warmer. The field that had once clearly shown the great division between the two little villages would now host their kindness towards one another.

The snow went from gentle dancing flakes to hefty stifling flakes. The wind howled and with each passing hour it was if more snow had been ordered to pound down on the two little villages. The coldness was debilitating. All trading had ceased because it became too hazardous to trudge through the snow. Each little village was grateful that they had shared supplies. There would not have been time to go to the usual neighboring villages before the

"White Hurricane" hit. The snow continued on the 12th, 13th, and 14th of March. No one had ever seen such snowdrifts. It was unbelievable.

The people of *Esperanza* and *Puente* had days to reflect on the kindness each had shown to one another. Each little village was in its own white tomb unable to move about. The people of *Esperanza* were convinced the wood from *Puente* really did burn longer. The people of *Puente* believed that the blankets made by the people of *Esperanza* were indeed somehow the warmest blankets in all of Appalachia. Wood that burns longer and blankets that are the warmest in the land take on new meaning when 55 inches of snow are outside your door. Contempt for the other village was replaced by gratitude.

The disturbing dreams of doves with drops of blood and tears were indeed transformed into the beautiful dream of doves peacefully flying due to one of the worst snowstorms in history. The Ramirez family succeeded, bringing peace with their prophetic gift. The two tiny villages that once balked at the divine gift of prophecy were now rejoicing over it. Yes, the people of *Esperanza* and *Puente* were actually happy *because* they built the bridge. The catastrophic weather taught them what they needed to learn, how to work together. Their hearts were light, no longer bogged down with generations of grudges. Each snowflake reminded their souls of how light harmony feels. Many had forgotten.

The deep snow was symbolic of the clean slate they now had. After the snow melted away, the towns people decided they wanted to end the division. They renamed the two villages into one name. The Ramirezes had helped build a bridge of hope. Now it is known as *Esperanza* Bridge.

The two teenage lovers looked over at the rocking chair and blanket. She said, "The blanket must be from *Esperanza*." He said, "The rocking chair must be made from the wood of Puente. It is wide enough for the two of us to sit in."

She peered over her shoulder to see if anyone was around and then she looked at him and said, "I wonder what would happen if we sat in the rocking chair together right now?"

A Deeper Look If You Wish

A greater look into history

- The Snowstorm of 1888 did shut down much of the east coast and is recorded as one of the worst blizzards in U.S. history. It occurred on March 11-14th in 1888. Sometimes it is referred to as the "Great White Hurricane."
- Hundreds of lives were lost.
- Winds of 45 miles per hour were recorded. There were also snowdrifts recorded as high as 50 feet in certain regions of Appalachia.
- The "Great White Hurricane" is attributed to being a major reason large cities on the east coast put their utility lines underground.
- The "Great White Hurricane" was so severe that on the other side of the Atlantic Ocean, the Yorkshire Herald in England reported on the impact the snowstorm had on the New York Stock Exchange.
- The weather right before the storm is recorded as being unseasonably warm.
- It was so springlike that on the 10th of March 1888, Walt Whitman submitted a poem which celebrates the coming of spring to the New York Herald. It was called the *"The First Dandelion."*

- This poem was published on March 12,1888 ironically during blizzard conditions.

A deeper look into the rest of the story

- Herlinda and Atanacio embarking on such an adventure in their 60's, is to highlight that age does not have to create a limitation on new adventures.
- Herlinda is pronounced air-linda because the H is silent. The name means gentle warrior and kind.
- Atanacio means immortal, not decaying
- The woodsy smell that reminded them of home is very deliberate. Smell is immensely powerful in bringing up memories because of the direct neurological pathway between it and the emotional and memory areas of the brain.
- Doves do have tear ducts.
- The valley is **U**-shaped for many reasons.
  o U-shaped valleys happen due to glacial erosion. The theme of erosion is present throughout the story.
  o U-shaped valleys create walls that are straight. This occurs because of non-bending glacier movement. The non-bending is characteristic of both villages.
- The pebbles are to remind all of us of the wide-reaching impact we can have and never be fully aware of how deep it really goes.

- The wooden rakes are symbolic of holding on to things. In this case-grudges.
- The pitchforks represent struggles and great laboring, mentally and physically. Mentally, the great laboring was all the hate and distain the feuding caused. Physically, building the bridge required great labor and struggle.
- The Ramirezes experience a **"South"** wind because this direction stands for warmth and growth. The South is considered the birthplace of "life". This also to highlight their ancestors are still bringing them life and the ways they brought new life into the region.
- It was the **"North"** wind because it symbolizes the cold between *Esperanza* and *Puente*.
- The thunderstorm is extraordinarily rich in meaning. Here are a few.
  o A thunderstorm usually is symbolic of chaos, difficulty, and negativity.
  o It foreshadows the "White Hurricane."
- *Esperanza* is to the **"East."** This direction symbolizes communication and new growth- which at the end they imbue these traits.
- *Puente* is to the **"West."** The symbolic meaning of west is going from complete ignorance into understanding and wisdom.
- The children are depicted as being more gracious. Children are often able to overlook

what adults struggle with. They are innocent because they did not make efforts to prolong the contention between the villages.

＋ The last name Ramirez is comprised of two meanings. The first one meaning "counsel" and the second one meaning "fame."

＋ A shaman is a person who is an intermediary bridging the natural and supernatural realms. They are said to be able to manipulate spiritual forces and use magic to cure illnesses.

＋ Lamacia's hair drug on the ground to help ground her into the earth plane and to soak up the energy of the earth.

＋ Lamacia has 13 necklaces because 13 can be symbolic because it symbolizes the death of the matter at hand and birth to the spirit. It is regarded as the passage on a higher level of existence.

＋ Lamacia put herbs and plants **together** because sometimes the most powerful result comes from working together.

＋ The next time she puts things in the fire **one by one** because sometimes the best result is achieved when things work independently.

＋ Lamacia **speaks** one time because there are times speaking achieves the most powerful result. She does not speak the next time because there are times **silence** achieves the most powerful result.

- Basil is well regarded in Ayurvedic medicine and traditional Chinese medicine.
- The two elixirs being combined is symbolic of both villages' participation in creating healing.
- Blankets are symbol of warmth and friendship. Blankets are used to create and seal relationships by some Native American tribes.
- Logs in this story are symbolic of all of the potential of warmth not yet released.
- The stage is made from wood from *Puente* to show them honor. Atanacio wears a blanket from *Esperanza* to give equal honor at the gathering.
  - There are multiple meanings of the embers and snowflakes. Here are a few.
  - The little embers of fire from the torches and dancing snowflakes are symbolic of how contrast can be beautiful.
  - It is also to demonstrate that two opposites can peacefully exist.
  - The embers are symbolic of the anger that filled the air by each village. The snowflakes are symbolic in how each town participated to bring peace.
- The one young brave man is in honor of all the people who have dared to be the "first" when no one else wanted to be.
- "The snow began pounding down onto the earth as if it were trying to convince

everyone how harsh things would become"
is also symbolic of all the harshness that had
been exchanged between the two villages.

- There are other deeper meanings throughout
the story not listed here. So, if you think you
found some you are probably right.

ABOUT THE AUTHOR

Andrea's fascination with languages started at a young age. Her ties to Latin and European culture provide a unique writing style. She takes the influences of these two different hemispheres and blends them together with the psychology of human nature. She has a Bachelor of Science in Psychology from Drury University and a Master's of Science in Counseling from Missouri State University. Consequently, she is keenly aware of the psychological dynamics within her writing. She enjoys weaving her life experiences into her writing. For more information go to womanwordweaver.com

Made in the USA
Monee, IL
04 February 2023

26221285R00022